Beauty and the Beast

First printing

PUBLISHED BY WINSTON-DEREK PUBLISHERS, INC.
Nashville, Tennessee 37205

Library of Congress Catalog Card No: 90-71857
ISBN: 1-55523-379-1

Printed in the United States of America

For Shannon

Beauty and the Beast

Retold and Illustrated by
Fred Crump, Jr.

TO SOW THE FALLOW SOIL

Winston-Derek Publishers, Inc.
Pennywell Drive—P.O. Box 90883
Nashville, TN 37209

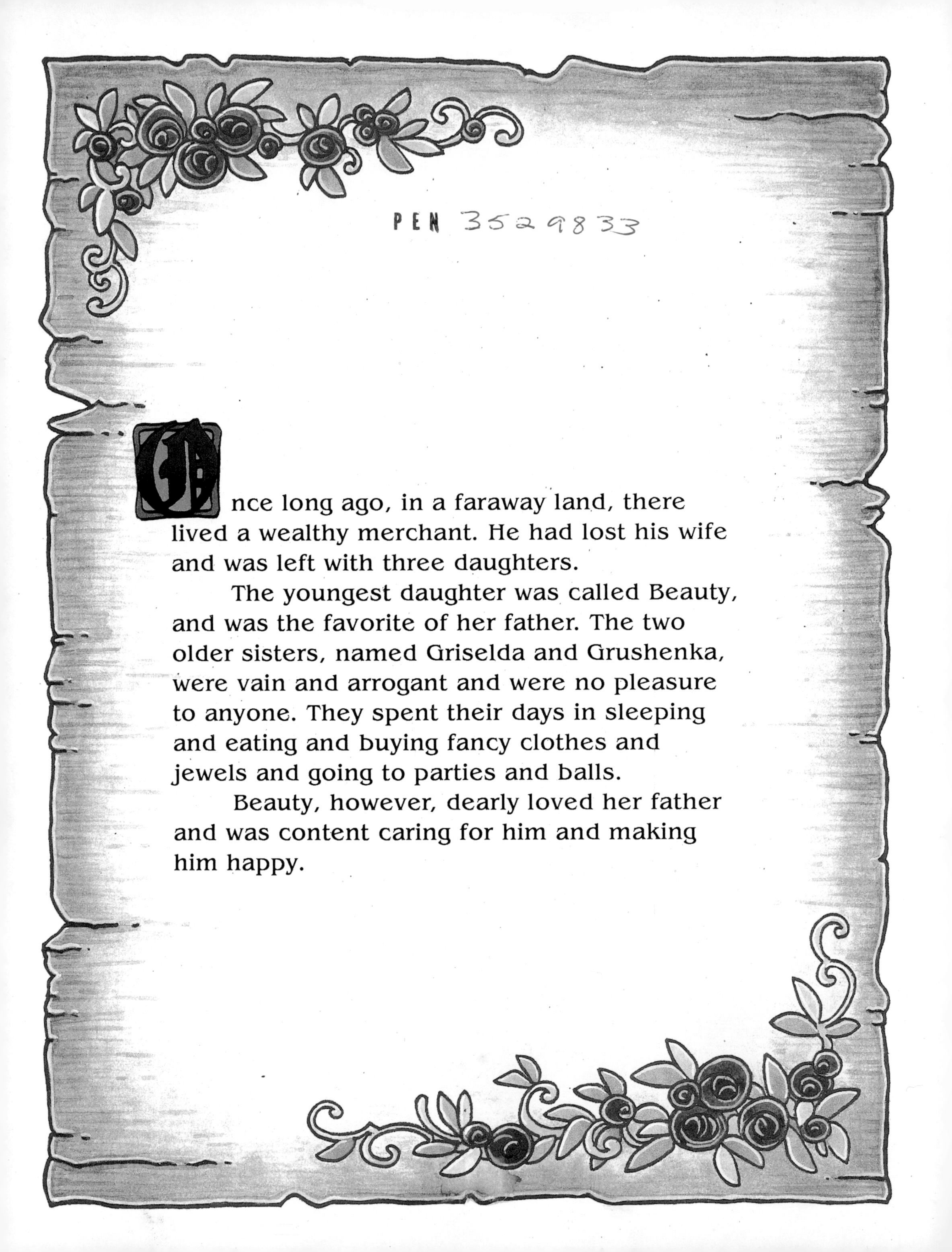

Once long ago, in a faraway land, there lived a wealthy merchant. He had lost his wife and was left with three daughters.

The youngest daughter was called Beauty, and was the favorite of her father. The two older sisters, named Griselda and Grushenka, were vain and arrogant and were no pleasure to anyone. They spent their days in sleeping and eating and buying fancy clothes and jewels and going to parties and balls.

Beauty, however, dearly loved her father and was content caring for him and making him happy.

One day misfortune struck. A fleet of ships belonging to the merchant sank in a storm. The good man lost all his wealth. He was forced to sell his fine mansion and possessions. The family moved to a poor house in the country.

Griselda and Grushenka were bitter about their reverse of fortune. Although reduced to poverty they continued in their arrogant ways. They refused to sell their fancy clothes and treated Beauty as a servant. Beauty tried to make things pleasant for her family, and her father came to love her even more.

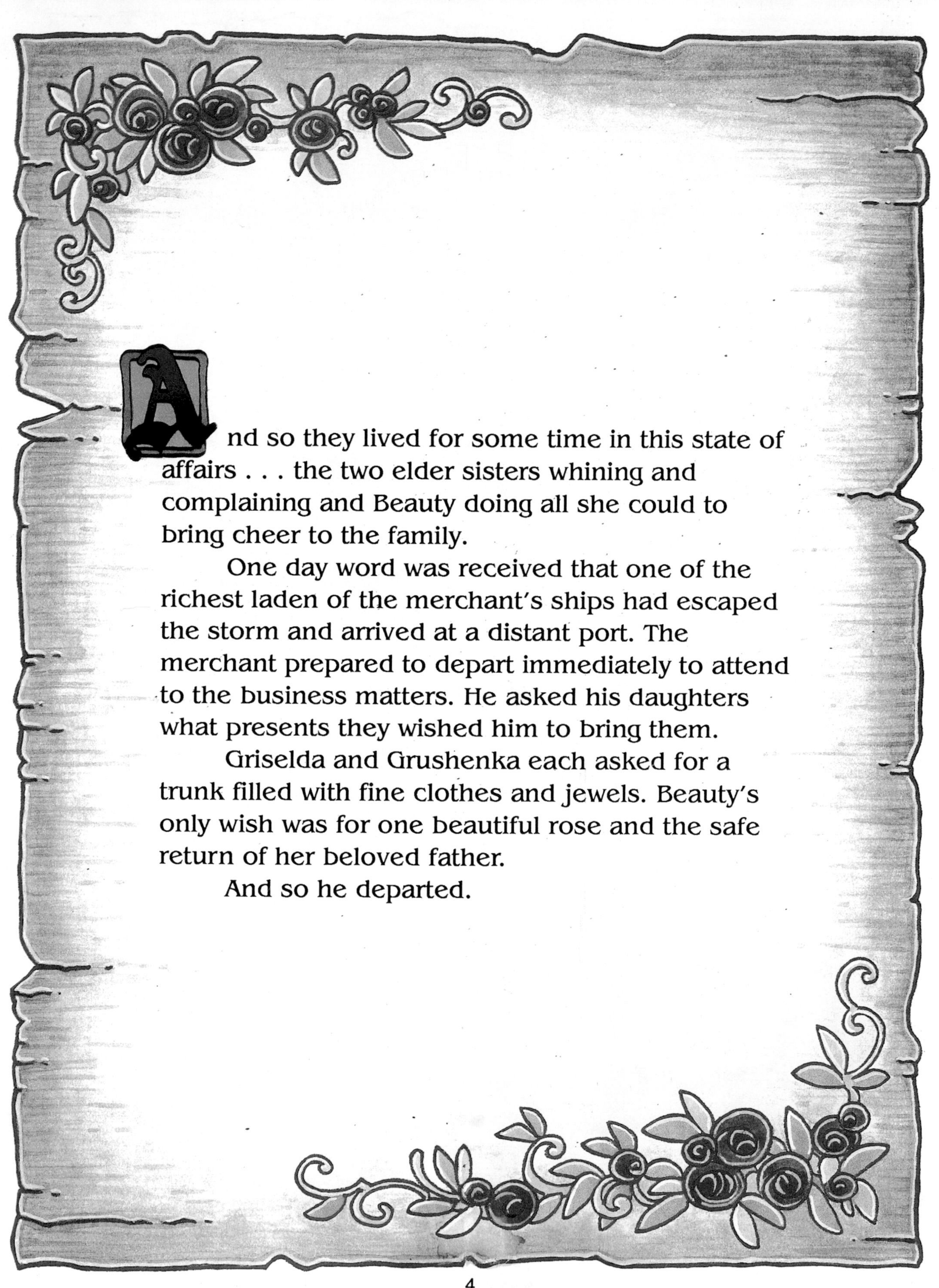

And so they lived for some time in this state of affairs . . . the two elder sisters whining and complaining and Beauty doing all she could to bring cheer to the family.

One day word was received that one of the richest laden of the merchant's ships had escaped the storm and arrived at a distant port. The merchant prepared to depart immediately to attend to the business matters. He asked his daughters what presents they wished him to bring them.

Griselda and Grushenka each asked for a trunk filled with fine clothes and jewels. Beauty's only wish was for one beautiful rose and the safe return of her beloved father.

And so he departed.

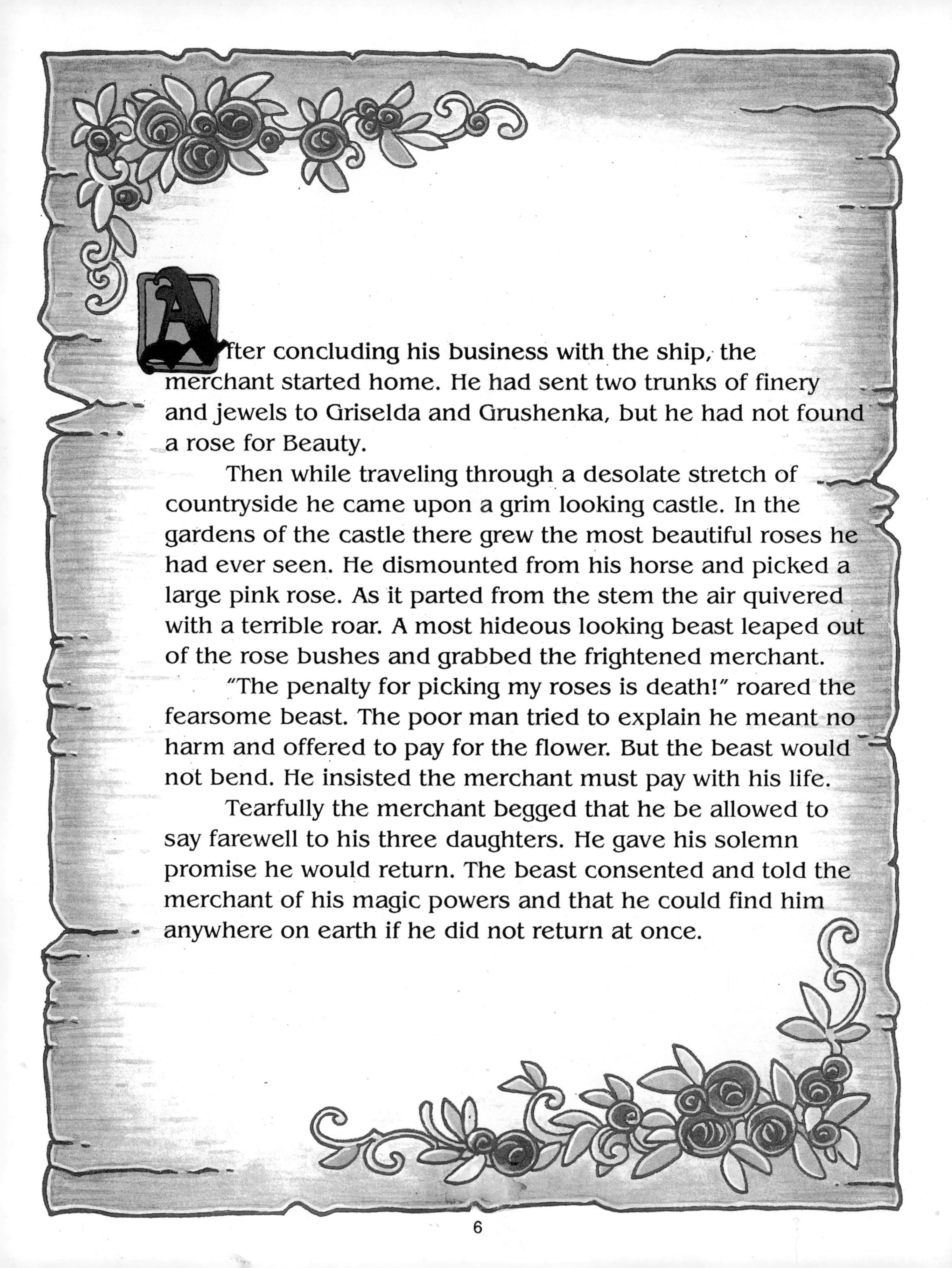

After concluding his business with the ship, the merchant started home. He had sent two trunks of finery and jewels to Griselda and Grushenka, but he had not found a rose for Beauty.

Then while traveling through a desolate stretch of countryside he came upon a grim looking castle. In the gardens of the castle there grew the most beautiful roses he had ever seen. He dismounted from his horse and picked a large pink rose. As it parted from the stem the air quivered with a terrible roar. A most hideous looking beast leaped out of the rose bushes and grabbed the frightened merchant.

"The penalty for picking my roses is death!" roared the fearsome beast. The poor man tried to explain he meant no harm and offered to pay for the flower. But the beast would not bend. He insisted the merchant must pay with his life.

Tearfully the merchant begged that he be allowed to say farewell to his three daughters. He gave his solemn promise he would return. The beast consented and told the merchant of his magic powers and that he could find him anywhere on earth if he did not return at once.

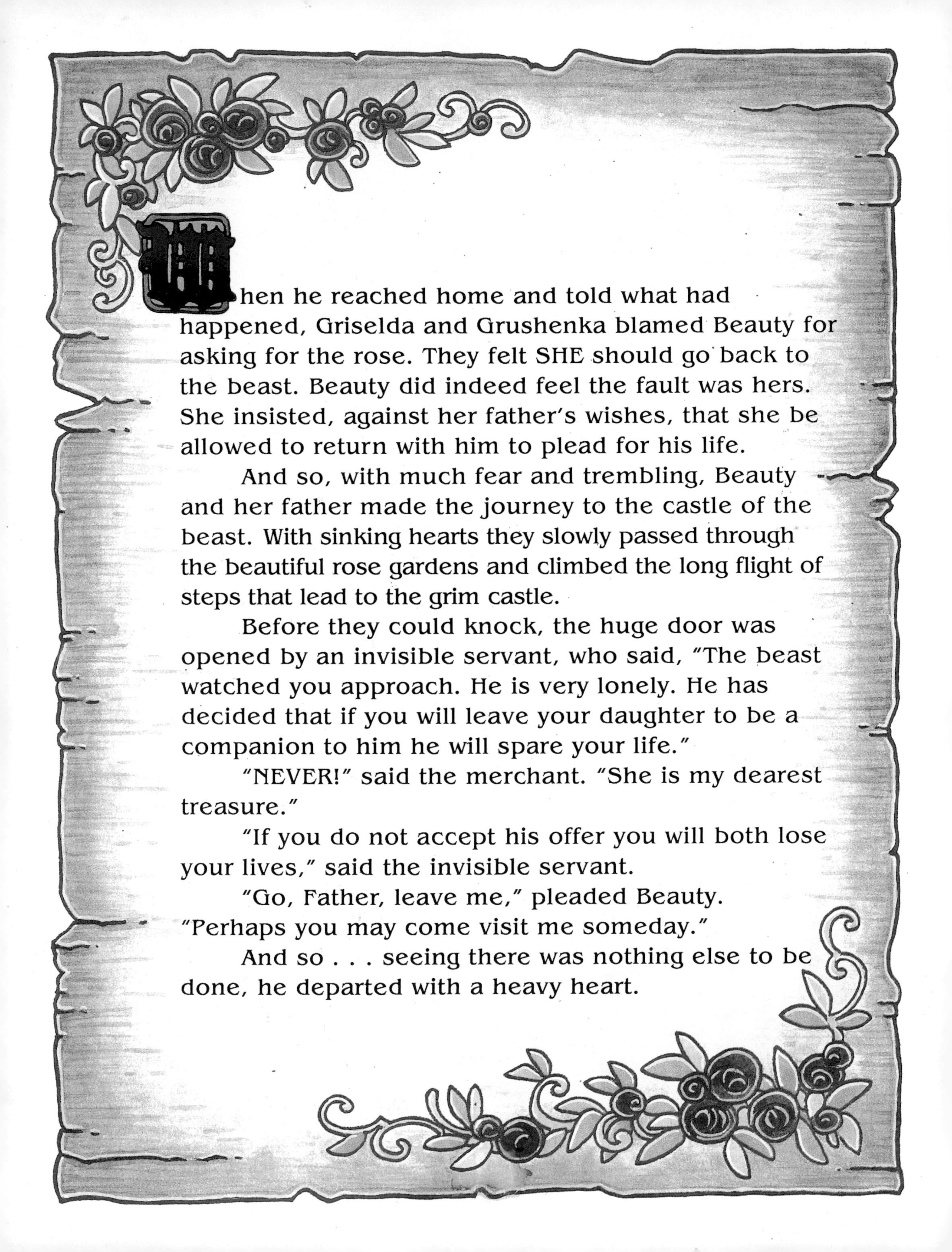

When he reached home and told what had happened, Griselda and Grushenka blamed Beauty for asking for the rose. They felt SHE should go back to the beast. Beauty did indeed feel the fault was hers. She insisted, against her father's wishes, that she be allowed to return with him to plead for his life.

And so, with much fear and trembling, Beauty and her father made the journey to the castle of the beast. With sinking hearts they slowly passed through the beautiful rose gardens and climbed the long flight of steps that lead to the grim castle.

Before they could knock, the huge door was opened by an invisible servant, who said, "The beast watched you approach. He is very lonely. He has decided that if you will leave your daughter to be a companion to him he will spare your life."

"NEVER!" said the merchant. "She is my dearest treasure."

"If you do not accept his offer you will both lose your lives," said the invisible servant.

"Go, Father, leave me," pleaded Beauty. "Perhaps you may come visit me someday."

And so . . . seeing there was nothing else to be done, he departed with a heavy heart.

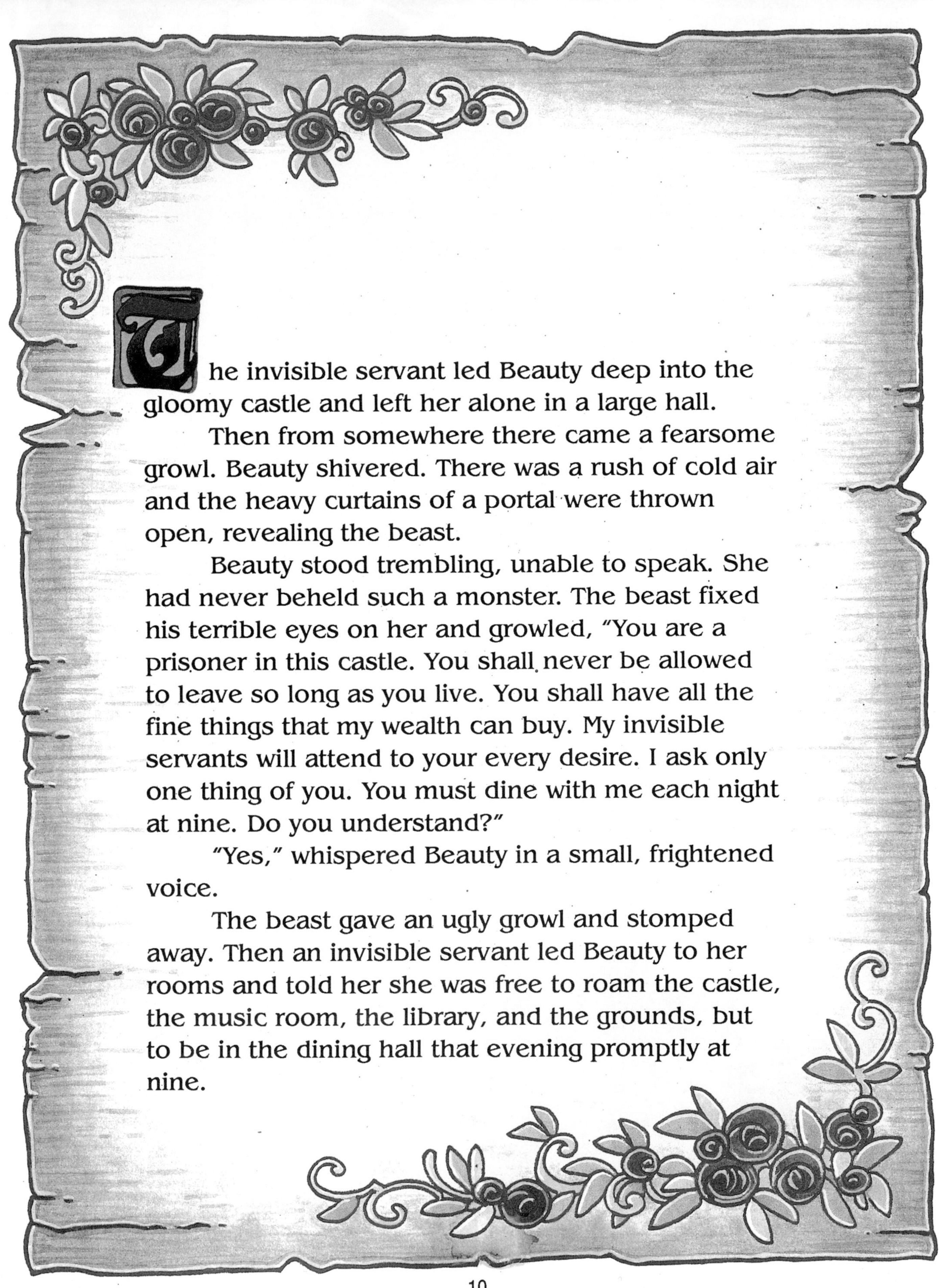

The invisible servant led Beauty deep into the gloomy castle and left her alone in a large hall.

Then from somewhere there came a fearsome growl. Beauty shivered. There was a rush of cold air and the heavy curtains of a portal were thrown open, revealing the beast.

Beauty stood trembling, unable to speak. She had never beheld such a monster. The beast fixed his terrible eyes on her and growled, "You are a prisoner in this castle. You shall never be allowed to leave so long as you live. You shall have all the fine things that my wealth can buy. My invisible servants will attend to your every desire. I ask only one thing of you. You must dine with me each night at nine. Do you understand?"

"Yes," whispered Beauty in a small, frightened voice.

The beast gave an ugly growl and stomped away. Then an invisible servant led Beauty to her rooms and told her she was free to roam the castle, the music room, the library, and the grounds, but to be in the dining hall that evening promptly at nine.

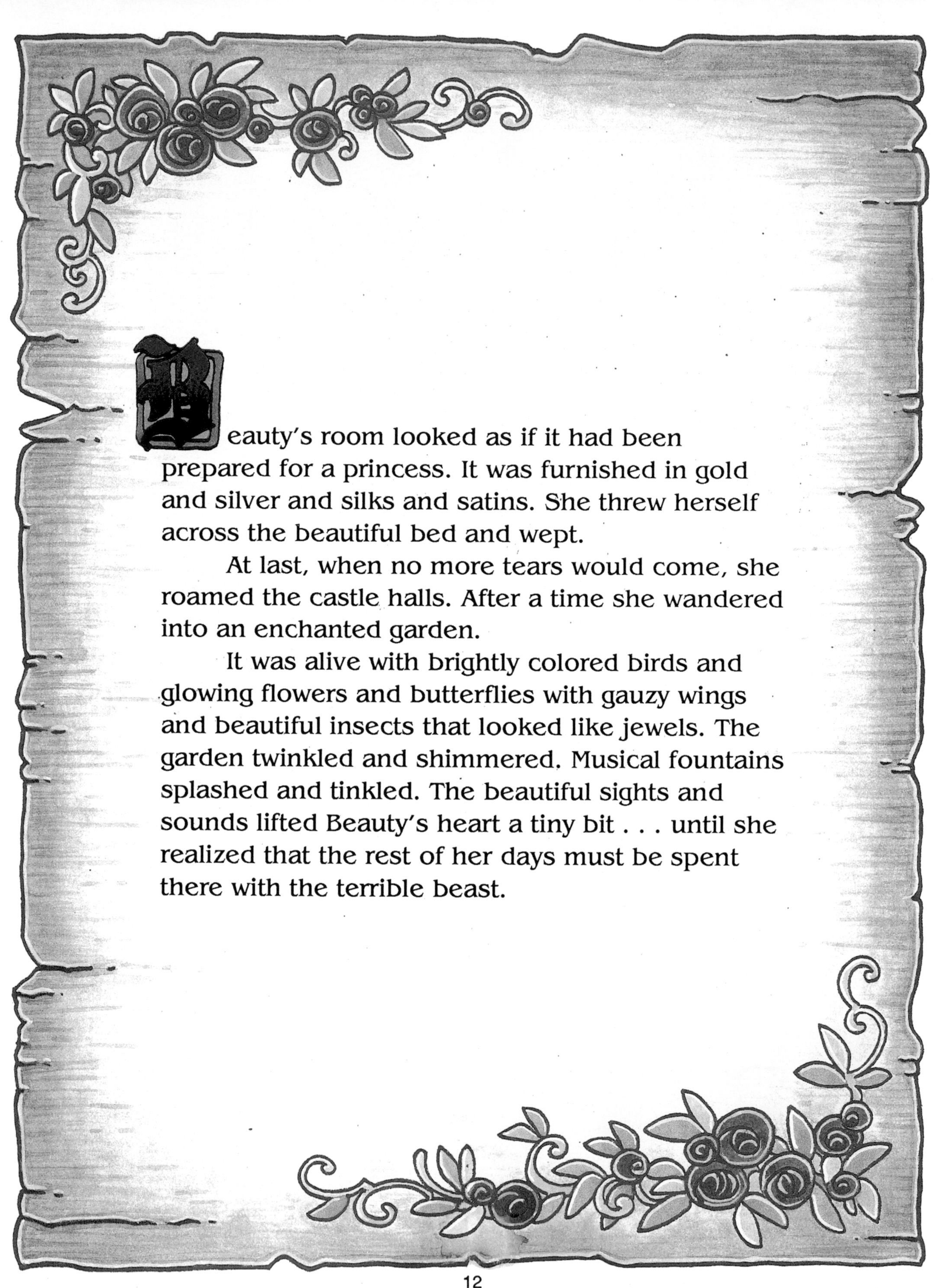

Beauty's room looked as if it had been prepared for a princess. It was furnished in gold and silver and silks and satins. She threw herself across the beautiful bed and wept.

At last, when no more tears would come, she roamed the castle halls. After a time she wandered into an enchanted garden.

It was alive with brightly colored birds and glowing flowers and butterflies with gauzy wings and beautiful insects that looked like jewels. The garden twinkled and shimmered. Musical fountains splashed and tinkled. The beautiful sights and sounds lifted Beauty's heart a tiny bit . . . until she realized that the rest of her days must be spent there with the terrible beast.

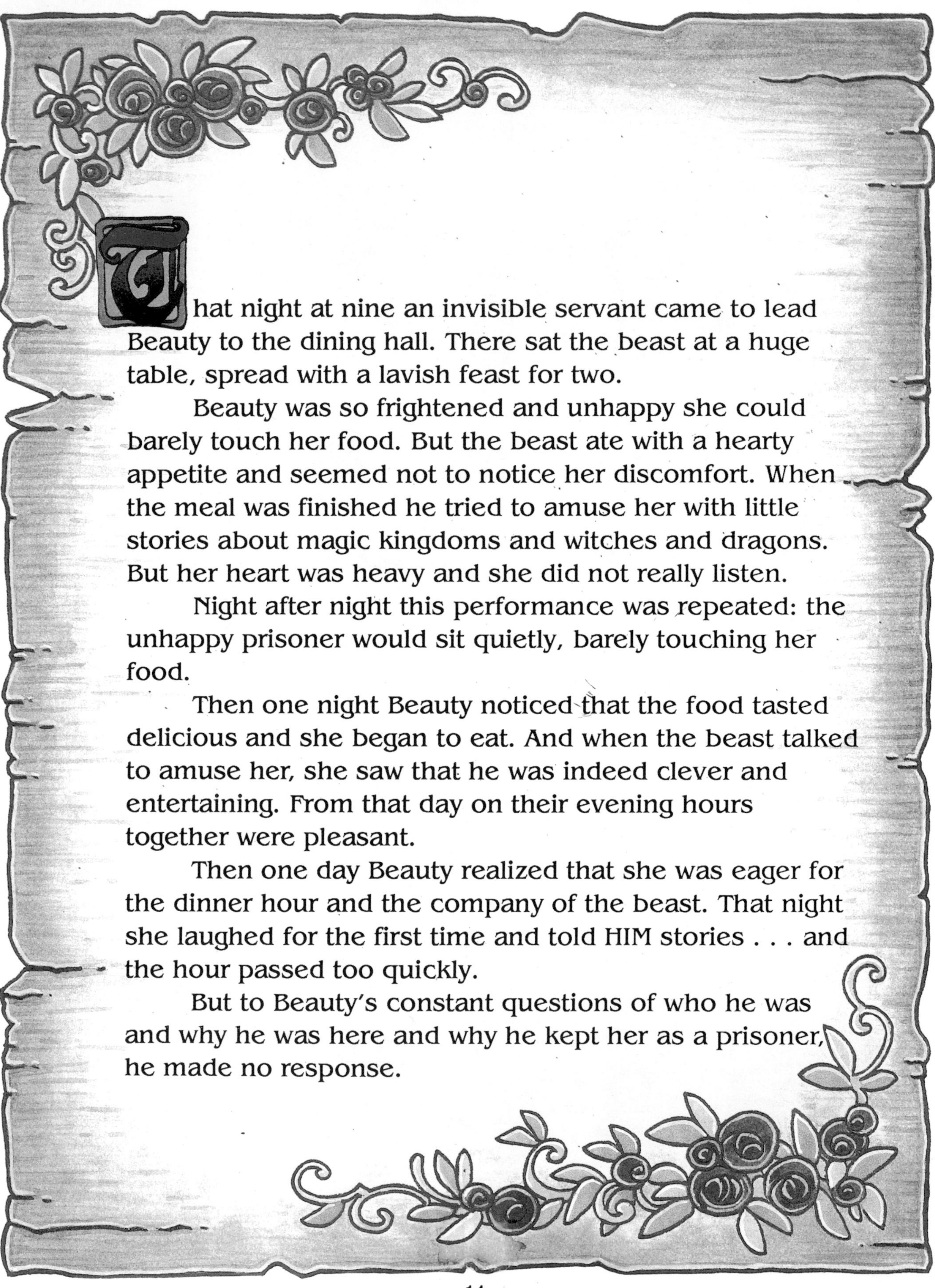

That night at nine an invisible servant came to lead Beauty to the dining hall. There sat the beast at a huge table, spread with a lavish feast for two.

Beauty was so frightened and unhappy she could barely touch her food. But the beast ate with a hearty appetite and seemed not to notice her discomfort. When the meal was finished he tried to amuse her with little stories about magic kingdoms and witches and dragons. But her heart was heavy and she did not really listen.

Night after night this performance was repeated: the unhappy prisoner would sit quietly, barely touching her food.

Then one night Beauty noticed that the food tasted delicious and she began to eat. And when the beast talked to amuse her, she saw that he was indeed clever and entertaining. From that day on their evening hours together were pleasant.

Then one day Beauty realized that she was eager for the dinner hour and the company of the beast. That night she laughed for the first time and told HIM stories . . . and the hour passed too quickly.

But to Beauty's constant questions of who he was and why he was here and why he kept her as a prisoner, he made no response.

To help keep her content, the beast gave Beauty a magic mirror. With it she could see her family, although they could neither see nor hear her.

The ship filled with riches had restored the merchant to a position of wealth. But although his two remaining daughters lived once again in luxury, they were still a pair of whining grouches . . . and he was unable to recover from his sadness over the loss of Beauty.

He grieved until he became ill. One night the magic mirror showed Beauty that her father was lying near death.

Beauty went to the beast and pleaded to be allowed to visit her father. She promised to return within a week. Three times the beast refused, and Beauty wept.

Finally the beast, moved by her tears, reluctantly consented.

"But be faithful to your promise to return within a week," he growled, "or terrible things will befall."

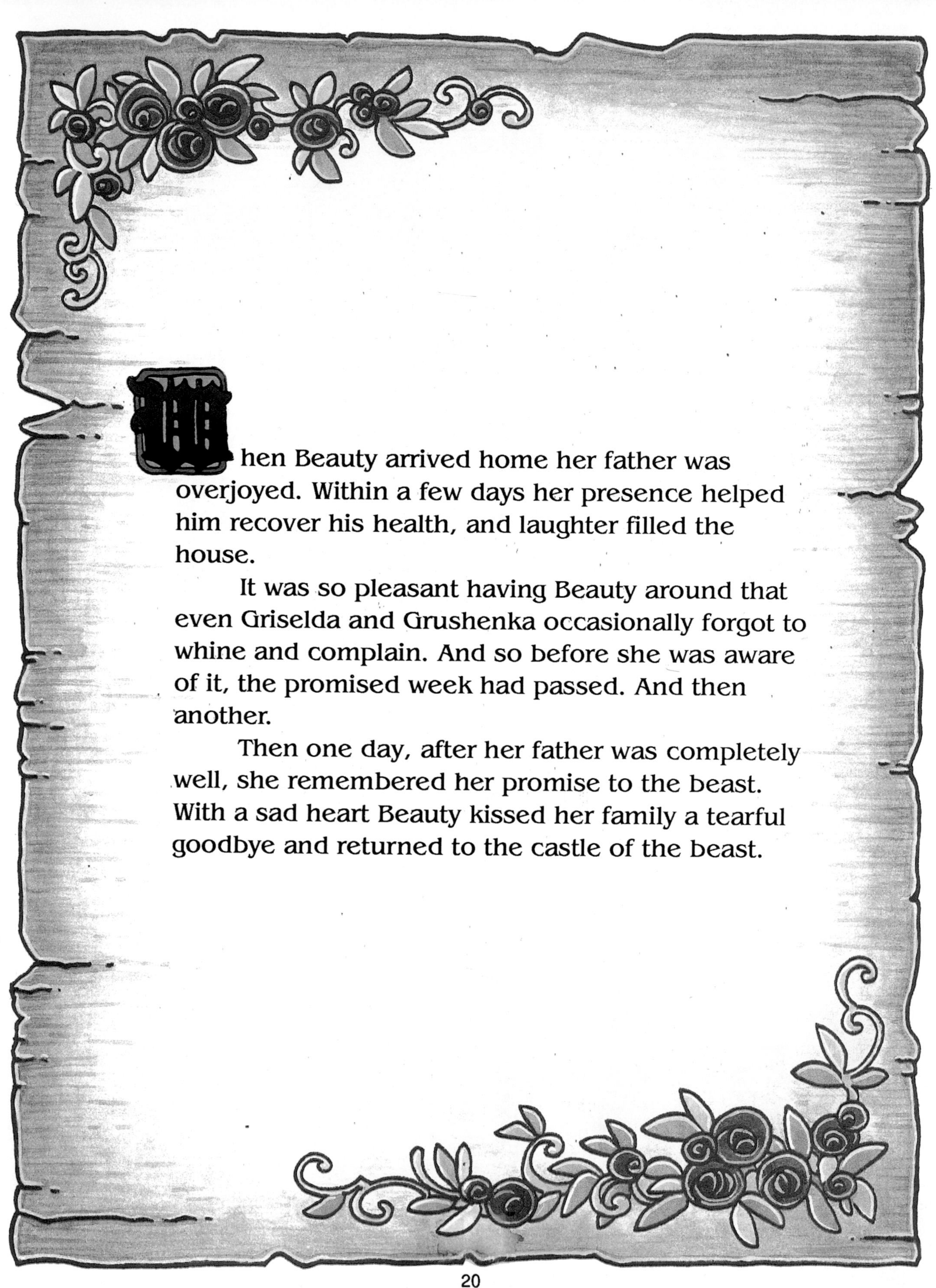

When Beauty arrived home her father was overjoyed. Within a few days her presence helped him recover his health, and laughter filled the house.

It was so pleasant having Beauty around that even Griselda and Grushenka occasionally forgot to whine and complain. And so before she was aware of it, the promised week had passed. And then another.

Then one day, after her father was completely well, she remembered her promise to the beast. With a sad heart Beauty kissed her family a tearful goodbye and returned to the castle of the beast.

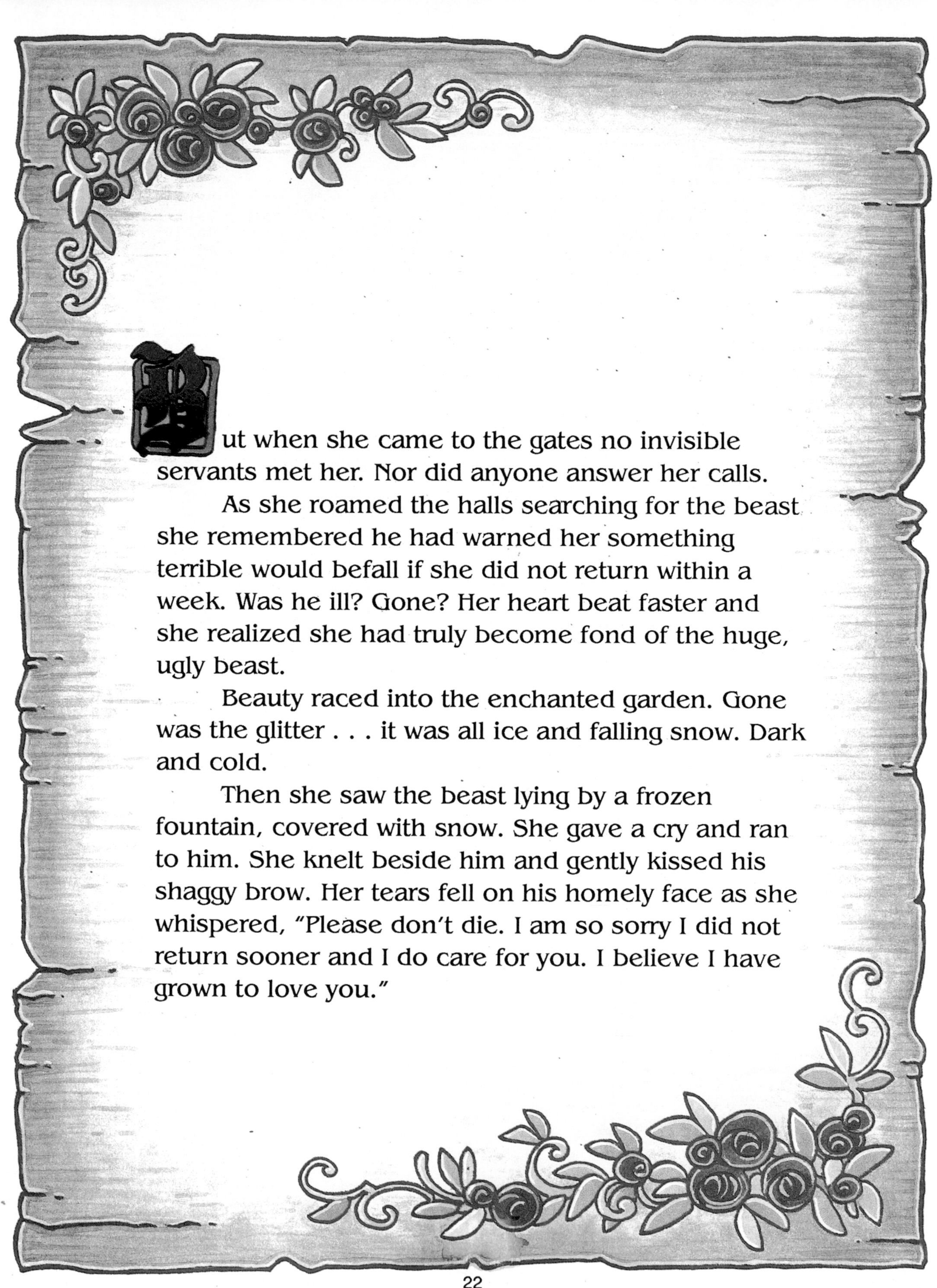

But when she came to the gates no invisible servants met her. Nor did anyone answer her calls.

As she roamed the halls searching for the beast she remembered he had warned her something terrible would befall if she did not return within a week. Was he ill? Gone? Her heart beat faster and she realized she had truly become fond of the huge, ugly beast.

Beauty raced into the enchanted garden. Gone was the glitter . . . it was all ice and falling snow. Dark and cold.

Then she saw the beast lying by a frozen fountain, covered with snow. She gave a cry and ran to him. She knelt beside him and gently kissed his shaggy brow. Her tears fell on his homely face as she whispered, "Please don't die. I am so sorry I did not return sooner and I do care for you. I believe I have grown to love you."

As she said these words the air glowed with twinkling lights. The snow and ice disappeared and the enchanted garden came to life.

But most wondrous of all, from the body of the beast there arose a smiling, handsome prince.

He said, "Long ago an evil magician cast a spell on me and turned me into a beast. Only the kiss from someone who learned to love me could break the spell. And . . . I have loved you since first we met."

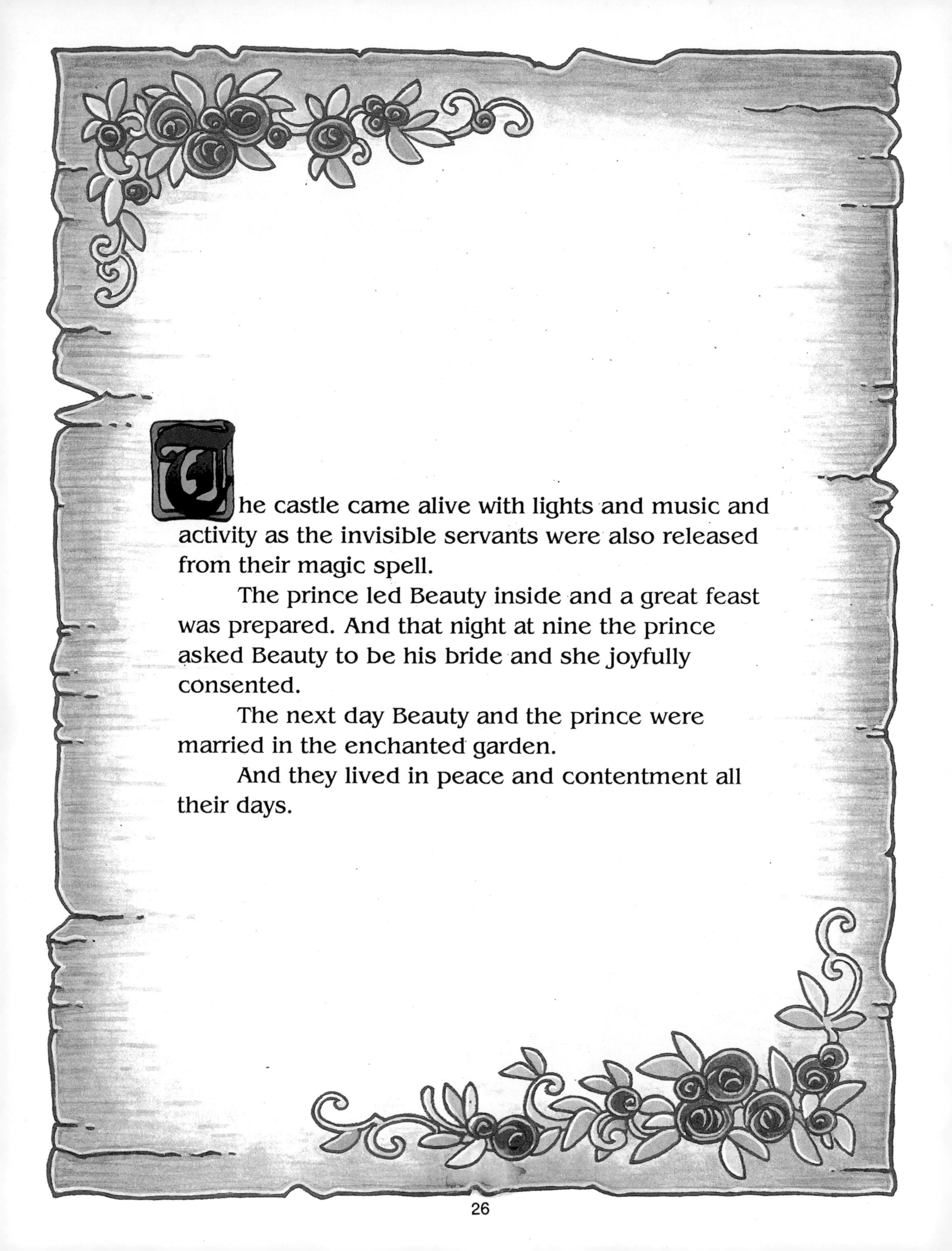

The castle came alive with lights and music and activity as the invisible servants were also released from their magic spell.

The prince led Beauty inside and a great feast was prepared. And that night at nine the prince asked Beauty to be his bride and she joyfully consented.

The next day Beauty and the prince were married in the enchanted garden.

And they lived in peace and contentment all their days.